M.O.M.*

*batteries not included

(Mom Operating Manual)

EXPRESS NONWARRANTY ALL EXPRESS OR IMPLIED WARRANTIES OF FITNESS FOR A PARTICULAR PURPOSE ARE HEREBY EXPRESSLY DISCLAIMED. THIS EXPRESS NONWARRANTY APPLIES TO DEFECTS RESULTING FROM NORMAL WEAR AND TEAR, PRODUCT MISUSE, AFTER-MARKET PRODUCT ALTERATIONS, OR FAILURE TO FOLLOW USE AND CARE INSTRUCTIONS.

by DOREEN CRONIN and LAURA CORNELL

atheneum books for young readers   New York London Toronto Sydney

This is the safety alert symbol.

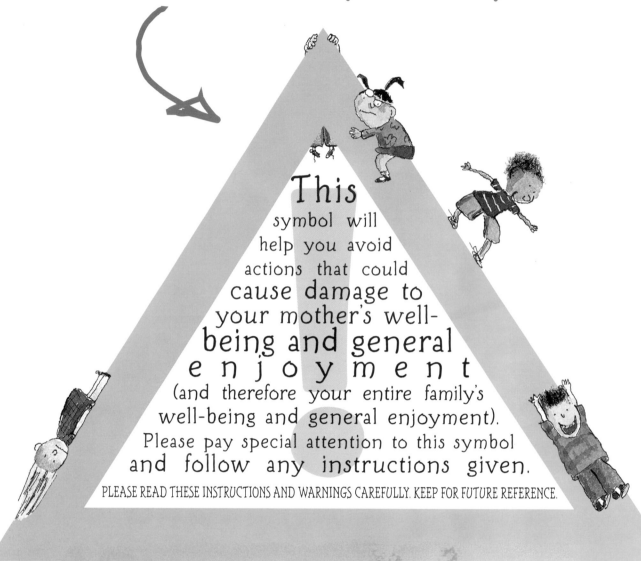

This symbol will help you avoid actions that could cause damage to your mother's well-being and general enjoyment (and therefore your entire family's well-being and general enjoyment). Please pay special attention to this symbol and follow any instructions given.

PLEASE READ THESE INSTRUCTIONS AND WARNINGS CAREFULLY. KEEP FOR FUTURE REFERENCE.

For Julia and Abby, with love, Mom
—D. C.

Thank you, my "extremely rare model" mom.
How lucky I am.
—L. C.

Atheneum Books for Young Readers · An imprint of Simon & Schuster Children's Publishing Division · 1230 Avenue of the Americas, New York, New York 10020 · Text copyright © 2011 by Doreen Cronin · Illustrations copyright © 2011 by Laura Cornell · All rights reserved, including the right of reproduction in whole or in part in any form. · ATHENEUM BOOKS FOR YOUNG READERS is a registered trademark of Simon & Schuster, Inc. · Book design by Ann Bobco and Alicia Mikles · The text for this book is set in Alghera. · The illustrations for this book are rendered in pen, ink, and watercolor. · Manufactured in China · 0711 SCP · 10 9 8 7 6 5 4 3 2 · Library of Congress Cataloging-in-Publication Data · Cronin, Doreen. · M.O.M. (Mom Operating Manual) / by Doreen Cronin ; illustrated by Laura Cornell. — 1st ed. · p. cm. · Summary: A guide to the care and maintenance of mothers, who are, according to the manual, "the most advanced human models on the planet." · ISBN 978-1-4169-6150-5 · [1. Mothers—Fiction. 2. Humorous stories.] I. Cornell, Laura, ill. II. Title. III. MOM (Mom Operating Manual). IV. Title: Mom operating manual. · PZ7.C88135Maaj 2011 · [E]—dc22 · 2010054145

Contents

Introduction

It is widely accepted that mothers are the most advanced human models on the planet. They are capable of superhuman energy, strength, patience, and creativity.

They come in many shapes and sizes.

They have various talents and skills, like cooking, singing, sewing, Olympic athleticism, and neurosurgery.

Years of research, observation, and time-outs have given science some very important guidance on the necessary maintenance and care of mothers for optimal performance. If you handle them correctly, tend to their basic needs (which are minimal), and refer to the care manual with regularity, your mom should be operating at peak performance for years to come.

3

Moms—
A Brief Historical Overview

PREHISTORIC Sludge Mom

Prehistoric Sludge Mom makes a tasty meal of unidentified sludge-like life-forms(?), "sludge" being the prevailing theme of that generation.

MOMS have been around for millions of years. They are the reason you are here. Keep this in mind at all times and act accordingly.

CAVE MOM

Cave Mom begins experimenting with clothing.

PILGRIM MOM

Cave Mom's life seemed almost easier than Pilgrim Mom's. Was Cave Mom more stylish? You betcha. You can almost hear them groan, "Turkey AGAIN?"

Hippie Mom

The REAL mantra of Hippie Mom: "I cannot spread peace and love on 3 hours of sleep a night." Surprised? Note clenched teeth and claw-like hands.

The torch has been passed to you.

Don't blow it. (And it's extremely hot—

don't touch it, stare at it,

or tease your sister with it.)

5

In modern times, a well-maintained, well-rested mom will look something like this:

THIS IS AN EXTREMELY RARE MODEL. YOU **DO NOT** HAVE ONE OF THESE.

It is more likely that you have one of the models shown here:

Failure to provide proper care and maintenance may affect your mother's overall performance, versatility, and dependability. Please note that ordinary wear and tear is perfectly normal. **Signs of ordinary wear and tear** include scratches, dents, fading, and occasional odor.

1) Reasonably Alert and Attentive Mom

Going

Semblance of a pleat — a good sign

6

going

gone

2) Pleasant Yet Fried Around the Edges Mom

or . . .

3) Barely Upright but Still Functioning Mom

Some concern

Cause for alarm

The kind and frequency of the maintenance services required are controlled by the number of hours in use (24/7 is normal), the season of the year, and how often you just do as you are told.

Daily Care and Maintenance

Regardless of the type of mom you have, there are many things you can do to ensure many years of trouble-free operation.

The Daily Basics

The essentials for a highly functional mom are Sleep, Nutrition, Exercise, and Water, or **SNEW** for short.

Sleep

To ensure peak performance, your mom needs eight hours of **peaceful, uninterrupted sleep** each night.

This will never happen, but it's important to set goals.

Check your mom's sleeping area and **remove**

any of the following:

Small children

Pets

Sharp, metal objects

Laundry

Cold pizza

If you can't remove the above, push them to one side of the bed and put a blanket over them.

Remarkably, despite their size, moms can sleep on as little as **three inches of bed**.

Science has no explanation for this.

3'

3"

Your mom is likely **not getting enough sleep** if:

1) She has packed you a

lunch of unsweetened

cocoa and a raw egg.

2) She has crawled into

the trunk of the car.

3) She is trying to lick

the bottom of her

coffee cup.

If any of these behaviors are apparent, you must insist that your mother take a nap, or find someone tall enough to pour her another cup of coffee.

Nutrition

It is extremely important that she get at least two well-balanced meals

a day from the "**ideal**" or "**acceptable**" categories below:

 IDEAL

Grilled chicken with vegetables, hearty soup with freshly baked bread, tuna salad on a bed of crisp lettuce

ACCEPTABLE

Ravioli from a can,

leftovers from your lunch box,

cold pizza removed from

her sleeping area

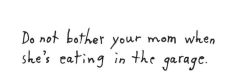

Do not bother your mom when she's eating in the garage.

! UNACCEPTABLE
Anything found under the **couch cushions** and/or **the seat of the car** (unless it's been there less than twenty-four hours, in which case it may have simply been misplaced).

NUTRITION
(continued)

EATING POSITIONS

The ideal eating position for your mother is **sitting up**, preferably at the **table**. If at all possible, she should be **stationary**. Although eating while moving is acceptable, it is not ideal.

 The following should be **discouraged**:

Eating while lying down (unsafe)

Eating while mowing the lawn (unsafe)

Eating while bathing (perfectly safe, but soggy)

(Much like a bottom feeder)

Note: Do not let your mother eat while operating an iron. In fact, do not let your mother operate an iron. Find something else to wear. Spread the word.

Exercise

Exercise is essential for your mother's peak performance. It also gives her a legitimate reason to put on her favorite sweatpants and leave the house alone.

RESISTANCE TRAINING

Weight training is essential for healthy bones and good posture. For maximum benefit, moms should train three days a week. Ideally, this will not include:

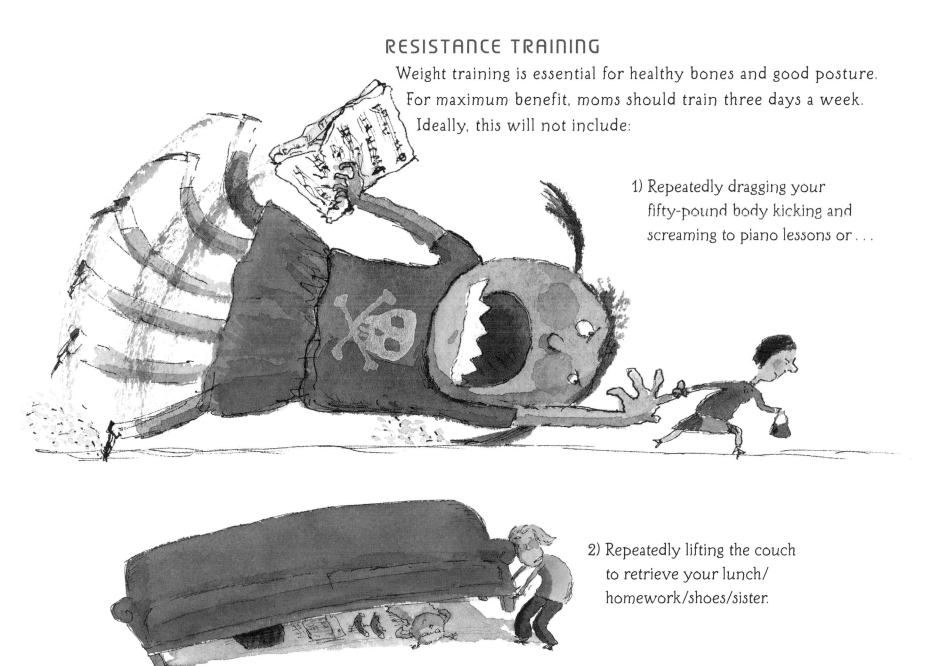

1) Repeatedly dragging your fifty-pound body kicking and screaming to piano lessons or . . .

2) Repeatedly lifting the couch to retrieve your lunch/homework/shoes/sister.

RUNNING

Moms need to run freely for a few minutes each day.

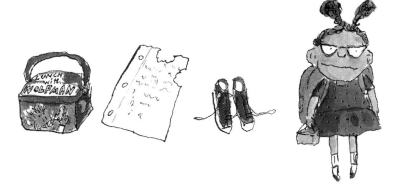

Ideally,

this will not include:

1) Running behind the school bus because you forgot your lunch/homework/shoes/sister or . . .

2) Running after the dog because he is eating your lunch/homework/shoes/sister.

Water

Moms should have an unlimited supply of **fresh, clean water** available to them at all times. If her hands are usually full, you may wish to install a drip bottle in the kitchen (or the garage, whichever applies).

If she is particularly active,
a **hydration helmet** may be necessary.

Grooming

Although daily bathing is not a necessity,
daily grooming is highly recommended.

Bath Night

Long, hot bubble baths are best. Hot showers are
also acceptable. Never use cold water or household
soap on your mother.

What's she doing?

⚠️ Under no circumstances should you try to clean your mother with a hose.

Not a Bath Night

Follow your mother's signals:

If she is sitting quietly,

it may be a good time for

her daily grooming. Gather

your siblings and gently

pick all pieces of debris, soil,

vegetation, and dried food

from her hair and clothes.

Do not eat your findings.

Hair

Mothers love to have their hair combed, brushed, and styled. There are also various accessories you may wish to experiment with.

Jaunty beret

Huge pink bow

Sparkly barrettes

⚠ Never give your mom a home perm.

Clothing

The vast majority of **moms** come with a **self-dress mode**. There is no override button. Keep your comments to yourself. Advise your father to do the same.

Teeth

There is no legitimate reason to check your mother's teeth.

This is normal for moms on the go.

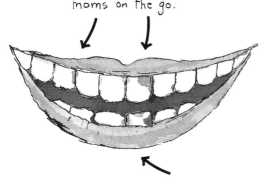

Outdoor Use

Years of engineering experience have made mothers perfectly suited for both indoor and outdoor uses.

Taking Your Mom Outside

Moms are highly portable. You can take them almost anywhere with little or no advance preparation or additional accessories. Taking them along with you also gives them brief exposure to natural sunlight, which they enjoy.

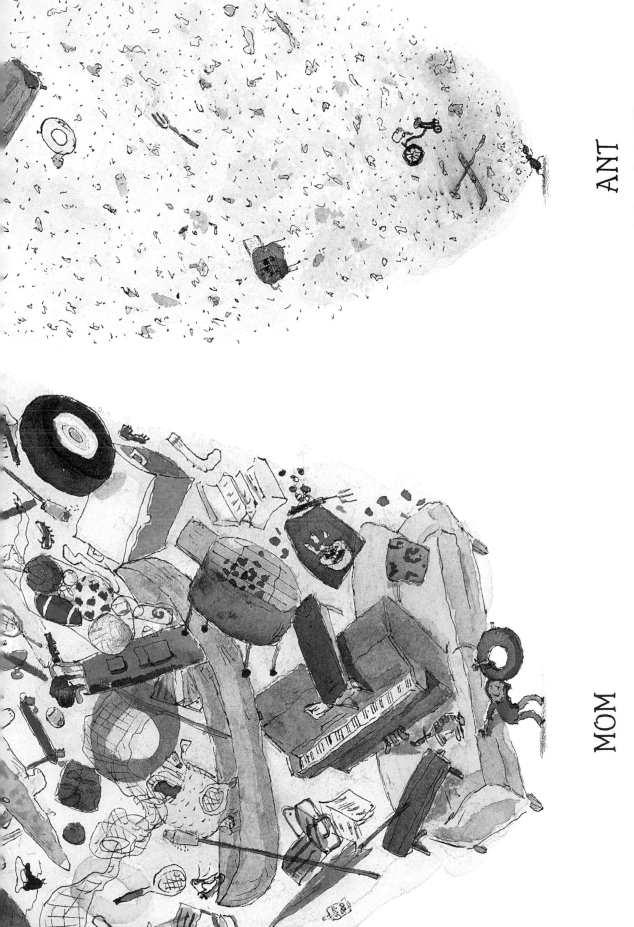

ANT

(enlarged 3,000%)

MOM

Packing

Moms can lift *many times* their body weight. This makes them extremely helpful in any outing that requires sports equipment, packages, small barbecues, and younger siblings.

It is important that Mom **balances the weight** properly.

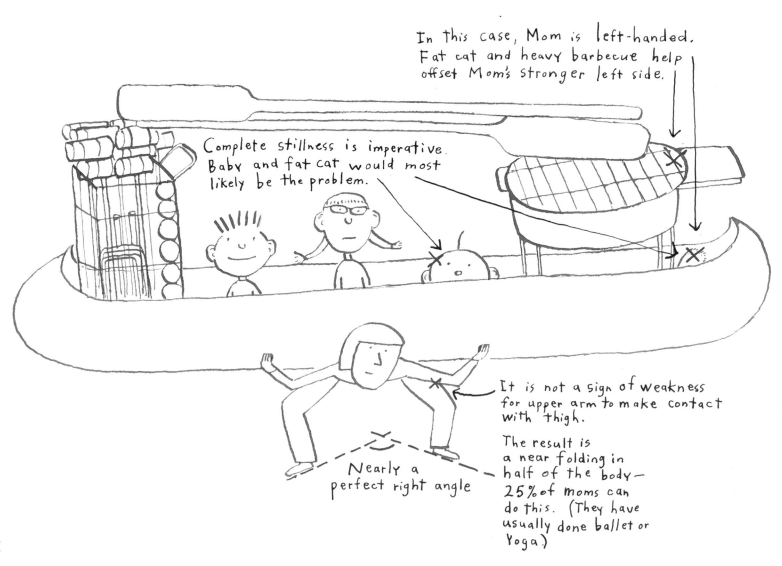

In this case, Mom is left-handed. Fat cat and heavy barbecue help offset Mom's stronger left side.

Complete stillness is imperative. Baby and fat cat would most likely be the problem.

It is not a sign of weakness for upper arm to make contact with thigh.

The result is a near folding in half of the body— 25% of moms can do this. (They have usually done ballet or Yoga.)

Nearly a perfect right angle

IMPORTANT SAFEGUARDS

1) Read all loading instructions carefully.

2) To protect against risk of electric shock, do not put your mother in water or other liquid while loading.

3) Keep hands, hair, and clothing away from your mother during heavy load operation to reduce the risk of injury to persons or damage to your mother.

4) The use of attachments not recommended or endorsed by your mother may cause fire, electric shock, or a very serious talking-to.

5) Not recommended for industrial use.

If your mother should **trip** or **fail to operate**, please check the following:

1) Is she accidentally attached to something

   (hair stuck in car door, jacket stuck in branch, etc.)?

2) Is she **awake**?

3) Unload your mother and let her rest for ten to fifteen seconds,

   then load her up again.

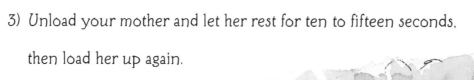

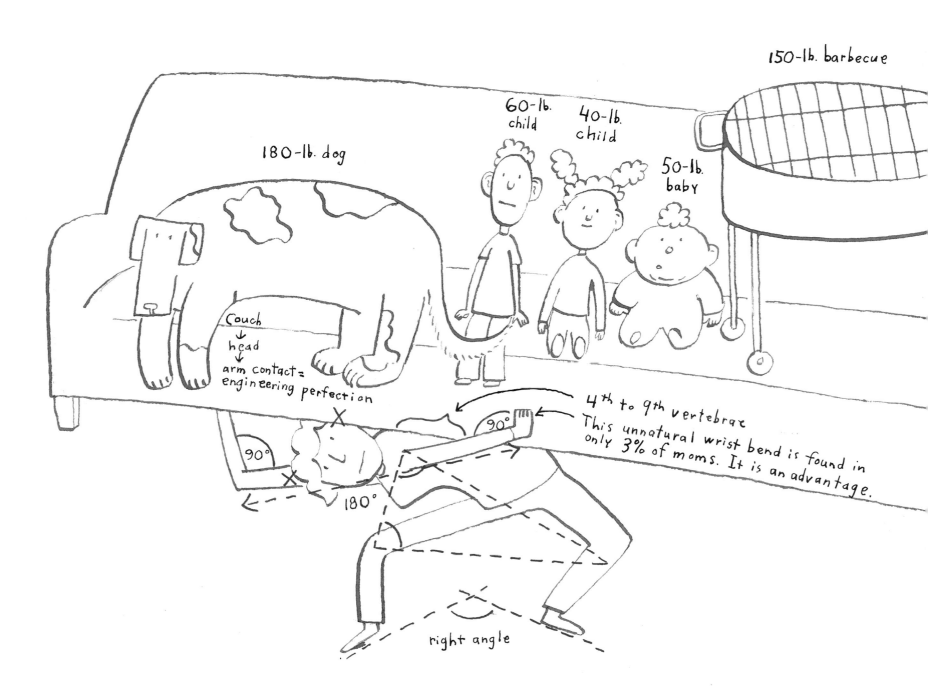

Note: Will not maintain fast speeds under heavy loads.

 Your mother may warm up during periods of extreme use. Under heavy loads with extended carry times, your mother may be warm to the touch. This is normal.

Transportation

ON THE ROAD

seat belts serve two purposes:

1) To keep you **safe**

and

2) To prevent your mom from **reaching behind her** while she is driving.

⚠ Though most efficient, this requires the opposite (WRONG) foot on the brake/accelerator.

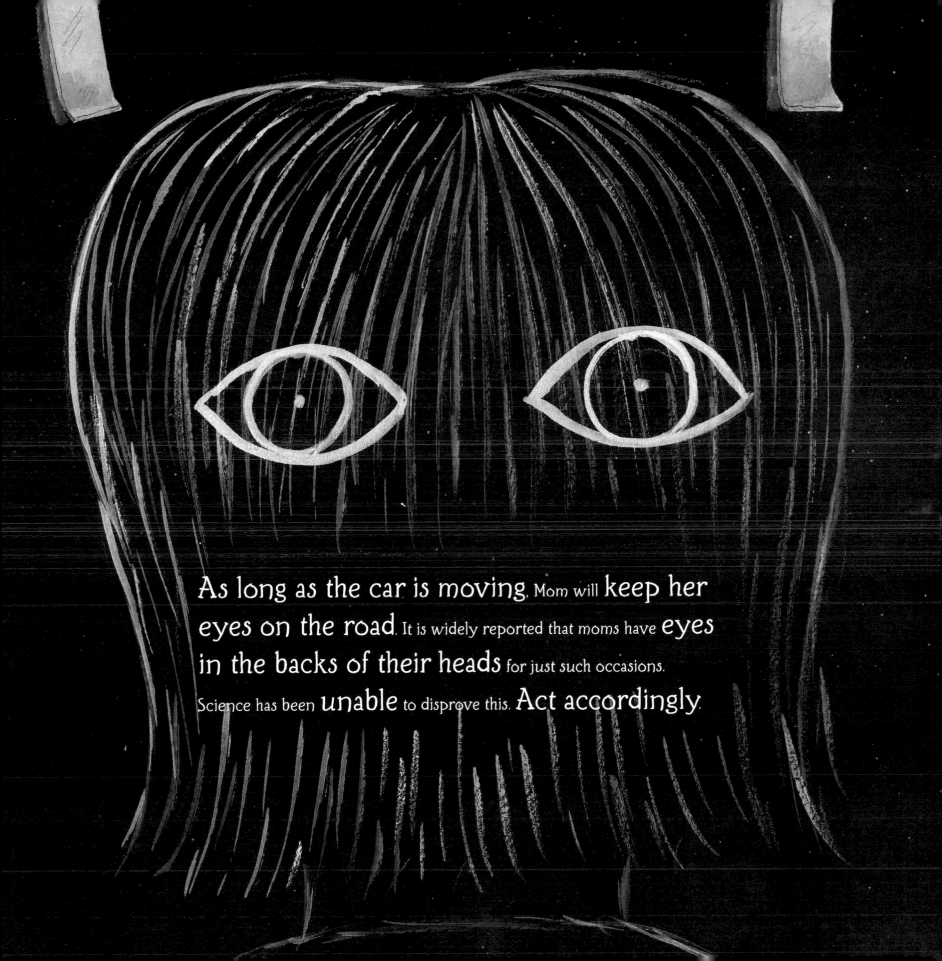

As long as the car is moving, Mom will keep her eyes on the road. It is widely reported that moms have eyes in the backs of their heads for just such occasions. Science has been unable to disprove this. Act accordingly.

Pulling over and turning the car around has been widely dismissed as a myth. It is not. Act accordingly.

34

Special Note

Do not wait until you are in bumper-to-bumper traffic to announce that you have to pee.

There has been more than one documented case of a mother handing a child an empty coffee cup in order to "take care of business."

Do **not** be that child. If you have siblings in the car with you, they will tell this story at your wedding.

TRANSPORTATION
(continued)

IN THE AIR

When the seat-belt sign is turned off and the captain announces that "you are free to move about the cabin," it does not apply to you. It applies to your mother. It is okay to **let her roam**. She can only get so far and the flight attendants will ensure that she claims you upon landing.

Unless instructed to do so by the flight attendants, under no circumstances should you look for, refer to, touch, or inflate the emergency vest. If you do, your mother will make you wear it for the entire duration of your trip.

MASS TRANSIT

Moms are easily transportable by subway, bus, or train.

Because there are no seat belts, your mom will have full range of motion.

Act accordingly.

BY CANOE

It's rare, but it happens. If you must travel by canoe, sit in the back of the boat. Your mom will be at the front of the canoe and unable to see you as she paddles. Listen carefully to instructions as to when to paddle and on which side. Ignore them completely. When your mom grows tired of traveling in circles, stop giggling and get paddling.

Troubleshooting

Moms are the most adaptable human models on the planet. They operate equally well in rain, snow, sleet, hail, and extreme heat. They can function with little or no sleep, little or no food, and little or no cooperation from the rest of us.

However, even this extraordinary ability to adapt has its limits.

The unfortunate result will be the

Malfunctioning Mom.[1]

It is often the result of poor maintenance, overuse, or lack of SNEW (see page 8). It is important to remember that if you find yourself with a Malfunctioning Mom, it may not be your fault at all.

It may be your father's fault.

---

[1] This is often referred to as "Cranky Mom." There is no alert symbol large enough to warn against use of this term out loud.

Minor Malfunctions

Unfortunately, none of the models presently in use comes with a flashing light to alert you to trouble. However, experience has taught us that **certain auditory signals** may indicate minor malfunctions.

HEAVY SIGHING

This is a deep breath that is exhaled with an unusual amount of **force** and may be accompanied by a **moan**. **Likely causes:** Are you drawing a mural on the wall with lipstick? Are you abusing your access to the duct tape?

Quick fix: Stop doing that.

GROANING

This is a **low**, muffled sound, often made through pursed lips. **Likely causes:** Did you forget to flush the toilet again?? Did you just walk through the living room carrying the garden hose? **Quick fix:** Flush the toilet and replace the hose immediately.

SNAPPING

This will be your mother expressing everyday language, but at **heightened volume** and **accelerated** or **unusual speed**.

For example,
"Put your shoes on, please"
may sound more like

Putyourshoesonplease!

Or

PUT your SHOES on, PLEASE!

Likely cause: You won't put your shoes on.

Quick fix: Put your shoes on.

EERIE SILENCE

Your mom is not making any sounds at all. She has a faraway look in her eyes.

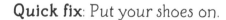

Likely cause: Overload.

Quick fix: Call Grandma, ask her to come get you.

42

If You Can Leave the Room

Should your mother be experiencing a minor malfunction, your best option is simply avoidance. Tiptoe quietly to another part of the house until the coast is clear.

clean = upwind

! If you are clean and lovely, you may proceed upwind. If you need a bath, a path downwind is your best bet.

dirty = downwind

If You Cannot Leave the Room

Camouflage can be very effective during minor malfunctions. **silence is key.** Use mud, grass, leaves, strips

of cloth, etc., to lower your probability of detection. Take your surroundings into account. If you are behind the sofa, a tall leafy branch is probably not a great idea.

If you come face-to-face with your Malfunctioning Mom, you must proceed with caution:

1) Do **not** run.

2) Back away slowly, speaking in a calm, monotone voice. You want to show her that you are being **submissive** and want to get out of her territory.

3) Do not turn your back. Stay **calm** and **quiet**, make no sudden moves.

4) Break eye contact. Do not stare into the mother's eyes, as this is a sign of **aggression**.

5) Climb a tree.

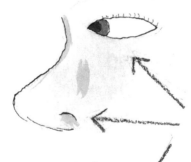

mom = grizzly

you = up tree

The instructions above can also be used if you encounter a grizzly bear in the wild. (Keep in mind that both mothers and grizzlies can be strong climbers.)

If you see this, escape is the only option.

Plan Ahead

In the event of a major malfunction, you will need a warning system, a rendezvous site, and a survival kit:

Warning System

If you are the first in your home to detect a major malfunction, you must warn the others. It is a good idea to work out a signal or phrase in advance:

"Agnes is bald."

"The Eagle has landed."

Or quite simply,

"Albuquerque."

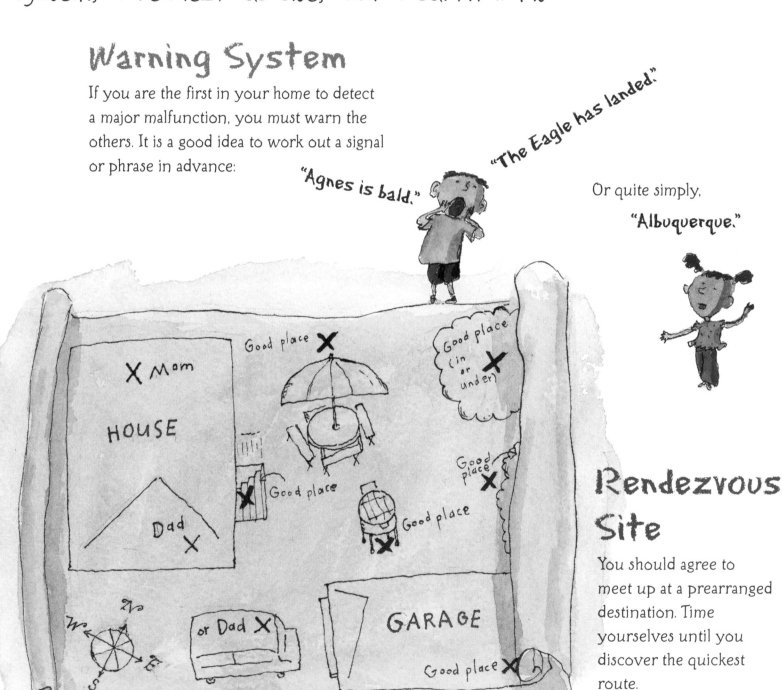

Rendezvous Site

You should agree to meet up at a prearranged destination. Time yourselves until you discover the quickest route.

Sustenance

85% Granola 100% Bar

literature

Lord of the Flies

hydration

93% H₂O

Sibling

Sibling

sibling

enticement

enticement

POW POW POW

POW

Giant Ziploc

In the case of a major malfunction, you may have to resort to self-care for as little as a few minutes or as long as a few hours. Be prepared. You should fill a Ziploc with a granola bar, a bottle of water, and a good book. Keep it in a cool, dry place. Grab it and head to the rendezvous site. Bring your siblings. If they are too big to carry, encourage cooperation with promises of cookies and cartoons.

Survival Kit

Reset

Major malfunctions are rare and are normally the result of improper use of your mother. The good news is, you can prevent them with proper behavior, cooperation, and good listening. Should you be incapable of any of the above, try playing the following mother-approved games:

The Quiet Game

The simplest of all games. Turn off the television and all other

electronic devices. Nobody speaks

for **five, ten**, or even **fifteen** minutes.

The Imagination Game

Turn off the television and all other electronic devices.

Do not poke/pinch/touch or acknowledge your brother/sister/dog.

Imagine that you are **a rock, a stick, a spoon**, or **a spool of thread**. Do it for as long as you can.

No matter what your older sibling tells you,

these are not

good games:

If All Else Fails

Sometimes a spontaneous song and dance routine can override the malfunction.
If you have time, rehearse. If you don't, just wing it. For example:

CRANKY PANTS

(sung to the tune of "Mary Had a Little Lamb")

Why do you wear cranky pants?

(Put thumbs in belt loops)

Cranky pants?

(Put hands on hips)

Cranky pants?

(Wag finger in front of you)

Why do you wear cranky pants?

(Raise arms to sides and shrug shoulders)

Breathe deep and count to ten.

Your mom will smile, laugh, cry, or snore.
She has successfully reset.

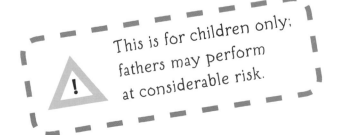

This is for children only;
fathers may perform
at considerable risk.

Final Note

If you have additional questions or concerns, please **contact** your **mom** directly.